THE
CHRISTMAS

by MARYANN MACDONALD

Illustrated by AMY JUNE BATES

DIAL BOOKS *for* YOUNG READERS

CAT

an imprint of Penguin Group (USA) Inc.

For Ann and Winston Ingalls, who love cats
—M.M.

For Katie
—A.J.B.

DIAL BOOKS *for* YOUNG READERS * *A division of Penguin Young Readers Group*
Published by the Penguin Group * Penguin Group (USA) Inc, 375 Hudson Street, New York, New York 10014, U.S.A.

USA / Canada / UK / Australia / New Zealand / India / South Africa / China
Penguin Books Ltd, Registered Offices: 80 Strand, London WC2R 0RL, England
For more information about the Penguin Group visit penguin.com

Text copyright © 2013 by Maryann Macdonald * Pictures copyright © 2013 by Amy June Bates

Library of Congress Cataloging-in-Publication Data
Macdonald, Maryann. * The Christmas cat/by Maryann Macdonald; pictures by Amy June Bates. * p. cm. * Summary: A cat living in a stable in Bethlehem purrs Jesus to
sleep the night he was born. * ISBN 978-0-8037-3498-2 (hardcover) * 1. Jesus Christ—Nativity—Juvenile fiction. [1. Jesus Christ—Nativity—Fiction. 2. Cats—Fiction. 3. Pets—
Fiction.] I. Bates, Amy June, ill. II. Title. * PZ7.M1486Ch 2013 [E]—dc23 2012005716

Manufactured in China on acid-free paper * 10 9 8 7 6 5 4 3 2 1
Designed by Jason Henry * Text set in Pastonchi * The artwork for this book as created using watercolor, gouache, and pencil.
The publisher does not have any control over and does not assume any responsibility for author or third-party websites or their content.

JESUS WAS BEAUTIFUL,
LIKE ALL BABIES.

And like all babies, he cried.

The night he was born, nothing Mary did could comfort him. She wrapped him in a warm blanket.

She fed him. She rocked him. Still, he kept on crying.

Every animal in the
stable tried in turn to
soothe him.

Doves fluttered down from the rafters, settling on the creaky stable door. They cooed and cooed, but they could not stop the baby from crying.

The cow mooed low, as she had done for her very own calf, but Jesus cried still louder.

The donkey brayed a lullaby, but
that made Jesus cry loudest of all!

Then a curious kitten crept out of the shadows. Step by careful step, he edged toward Jesus. Reaching Mary's feet, he crouched, wiggled his back, and pounced lightly onto her lap.

Rubbing his tiny nose against the back of Mary's hand, the kitten showed that he too wanted his turn to soothe the baby. Mary opened her shawl. The kitten edged in and nuzzled Jesus's neck. Then he began to purr, a calm, contented purr that came from deep inside.

Jesus's tiny hand touched the kitten, and
his crying grew softer . . . and softer and softer.
Soon it stopped. The purring faded away too.

And in the blessed silence that followed, every tired creature in the stable was soon sleeping soundly in the starlight.

The babies grew close as two creatures can be. Before long,
the kitten became a cat. Jesus watched him as he chased butterflies
in the tall grass and climbed high in the fig tree.

And when Mary put Jesus down to rest in his cradle, it was the cat's turn to watch over the baby and purr him to sleep.

One day, an angel came to warn Joseph that terrible King Herod was looking for the baby Jesus. Jealous Herod had heard rumors about Jesus, that this baby would one day be king. Herod's soldiers, the angel said, were racing toward Bethlehem, hoping to find the baby Jesus and destroy him. To escape, the little family would have to flee on their donkey into Egypt— right away! It would be safest to travel quietly at night, in the darkness, when the soldiers could not see them.

"Hurry, Mary!" said Joseph. "We must leave now, this very night."
Rushing, Mary and Joseph packed and loaded what little they
could on their donkey.

"Where is Jesus's cat?" Mary asked, just before the sun went down. "We must find him!" So Mary and Joseph combed through the tall grass, searched the shadows near the fire and looked high in the branches of the fig tree. But the cat was nowhere to be found.

"We can't leave him behind!" cried Mary.

"We must," said Joseph. "It's too dangerous to stay here even one day longer." So just as the sun set on the hills behind Bethlehem, the little family set off on their journey.

The desert air was chilly. Mary held Jesus close, hoping the rocking gait of the donkey would lull him to sleep. But Jesus needed his cat. He clenched his small fists and screamed.

Campfires glowed on the nearby hillside. Were Herod's soldiers sheltering there with their swords? What would they do if they heard Jesus's cries? "I wish the cat was with us," Mary whispered to Joseph, but Joseph only nodded, his eyes constantly scanning the horizon.

But the cat was with them after all! To make sure he wasn't left behind, he had hidden in the basket tied to the donkey's warm flank. When he heard Jesus crying, he woke up and began to wail. Jesus shrieked with delight, reaching toward the basket with chubby arms. With one strong leap, the cat jumped into them.

"Shush, shush," whispered Mary as she cuddled the squirming, licking, loving friends together. When at last the two settled down, the cat again began to purr.

The rhythmic rumbling, as always, soothed the baby, and Jesus fell sound asleep. Inside Mary's shawl, he and his pet curled closer together, keeping each other warm as the donkey carried them far from Herod's soldiers and their awful swords, far away to the safe land of Egypt. Love had saved them.

The cat loved the baby Jesus, as only a child's cat can. And Jesus loved him back, as only a cat's child can.

For of all the cats and all the children everywhere, they were meant for each other . . . from the very first Christmas night, in the bright starlight.

AUTHOR'S NOTE

Leonardo da Vinci loved to draw *La Madonna del Gatto*, or the Madonna of the Cat. He made many drawings of her in 1480 and 1481. In the drawings, the chubby child Jesus is depicted holding, stroking, and playing with a cat.

Legend tells about a cat living in the stable in Bethlehem who purred Jesus to sleep the night he was born. If this were true, the cat might have become Jesus's pet. Meeting as they did that Christmas, the two might have had a special bond.